LITTLE MISS CHRISTMAS

Roger Hargreaves

Original concept by
Roger Hargreaves

Written and illustrated by
Adam Hargreaves

Little Miss Christmas lives in an igloo at the
North Pole, next door to her uncle, Father Christmas,
a long, long way from her brother, Mr Christmas.

Little Miss Christmas works for Father Christmas.
Her job is wrapping all the presents before Father
Christmas delivers them on Christmas Eve.

As you might imagine, there are an awful lot of
presents to wrap – it takes her all year long.
And as much as Little Miss Christmas loves her job,
there are times when wrapping presents day in and
day out can get a bit boring.

Last year, after nearly a whole year buried in wrapping paper and sticky tape, Little Miss Christmas decided that she deserved a holiday.

She had nearly finished wrapping all the presents, and thought that it would not do any harm for Father Christmas to wrap the last few himself.

To make it easier for him, she rang her brother at the South Pole and asked him to come and help.

Mr Christmas flew up to the North Pole in his magic, flying teapot on the day Little Miss Christmas left for her holiday.

"I won't be back until the day before Christmas Eve, so you have to make sure you finish wrapping the last of the presents," Little Miss Christmas reminded them just before she boarded her plane.

"Don't worry," boomed Father Christmas. "We've got plenty of time! We'll have them all wrapped long before you return."

The next morning, after a breakfast of Christmas pudding on toast, Father Christmas led Mr Christmas into the wrapping room and they set to work.

"This isn't going to take any time at all," said Father Christmas an hour later. "In fact, we've got plenty of time left. How about a game of golf?"

"Good idea," said Mr Christmas.

And so the two of them played golf for the rest of the day.

The following morning, they settled down to work.
But after an hour, Father Christmas piped up again,
"How do you fancy going reindeer racing?
We've got plenty of time left to do this."

"Good idea," agreed Mr Christmas.

And the two of them spent the rest of the day
racing reindeer across the ice.

The next day, they did not even reach the wrapping room.

"We've still got plenty of time to finish that wrapping. Shall we go fishing today?" suggested Father Christmas at breakfast.

"Good idea," said Mr Christmas, eagerly.

And so it continued.

While Little Miss Christmas lay on a beach in the Christmas Islands (where else?!), blissfully unaware of what was going on, Father Christmas and Mr Christmas were spending a lot of time having fun and very little time wrapping presents.

So you will not be surprised to learn that the wrapping had not been finished by the time Little Miss Christmas returned from her holiday.

"What have you two been doing all this time?" exclaimed Little Miss Christmas, when she saw the huge pile of unwrapped presents.

Father Christmas and Mr Christmas sheepishly studied their feet, unable to look Little Miss Christmas in the eye.

"How are we ever going to get all this done by tomorrow evening?" she continued, angrily.

It was then that she suddenly had an idea.

A brilliant idea.

"We can ask all the Mr Men and Little Misses to help us! And you can go and pick them up in your teapot!" she cried, pointing at Mr Christmas.

By teatime, Mr Christmas had collected as many of the Mr Men and Little Misses as he could find, and brought them to the North Pole.

They all worked right through the night, although Little Miss Christmas had to be careful about which jobs she gave them.

Mr Bump was only allowed to wrap teddy bears because he kept breaking the other presents he was given.

And Little Miss Bossy had to keep a careful eye on Little Miss Naughty, to stop her wrapping nasty surprises in her presents.

Not everything quite went to plan.

Mr Muddle kept writing "Happy Easter" on the labels.

And Little Miss Helpful tried very hard to be helpful, but got into a lot of trouble with the sticky tape.

Mr Forgetful kept forgetting to put presents in his parcels.

And there was no mistaking the presents wrapped by Mr Messy!

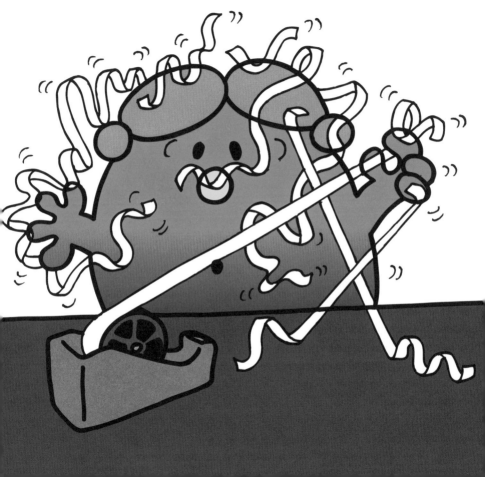

However, by lunch time on Christmas Eve, all the presents were wrapped and labelled and packed away in Father Christmas's sleigh.

"Thank you so much," said Little Miss Christmas to everyone. "I don't know what we would have done without your help. There would have been a lot of empty spaces under a lot of Christmas trees. Now we just need Father Christmas! Has anyone seen him?"

But nobody had.

Eventually, Little Miss Christmas found him playing cards – with Mr Christmas, of course!

"Quick, quick!" she cried. "You're going to be late!"

"Don't worry, don't worry," chuckled Father Christmas.

"We've got plenty of time!"

In the spring of 1588 King Philip II of Spain sent an armada, a huge fleet of ships, to conquer England. But the English, led by men like Francis Drake, were waiting to defend their country from a Spanish invasion.

The battles that followed and the sad end of the once-proud Spanish fleet are described in this beautifully illustrated book.

For Victoria

Acknowledgments

The author and the publishers would like to thank Hugh Speers for his help in the preparation of this book and the following for permission to use illustrative material:
R W Ditchfield maps 25, 38; Marc Jasinski 41 top; by kind permission of the Marquess of Tavistock and the Trustees of the Bedford Estates 42; Colin Martin 3, line drawing 18/19; Mary Evans Picture Library 7 top; The Mary Rose Trust 15, 16, 17, 19; Anne Matthews line drawing 10; The National Maritime Museum, London back cover, 5 top and bottom, 14, 24 top, 26, 27 top and bottom, 28, 29, 30/31, 34, 43 top (2); National Portrait Gallery 6 top; The National Trust 6 bottom; Northern Ireland Tourist Board 39 top and bottom; Plymouth City Museum and Art Gallery 43 bottom; Scottish National Portrait Gallery 7 bottom; St Faith's Church, Gaywood 35; Ulster Museum 4, 12, 18, 19 bottom, 20(2), 21, 23, 36, 40, 41 bottom.
Designed by R W Ditchfield.

British Library Cataloguing in Publication Data

Speers, Sheela
    The Spanish Armada.
    1. England. War with Spain, 1588.
    Spanish Armada – For children
    I. Title   II. Bisby, Harold   III. Dennis, Peter, *1950*–
    942.05′5

    ISBN 0-7214-1093-6

First edition

Published by Ladybird Books Ltd Loughborough Leicestershire UK
Ladybird Books Inc Auburn Maine 04210 USA
© LADYBIRD BOOKS LTD MCMLXXXVIII

Printed in England

The
Spanish
Armada

written by SHEELA SPEERS

with illustrations by HAROLD BISBY
and PETER DENNIS

Ladybird Books

Thomas de Granvela

Four hundred years ago, in the spring of 1588, a young nobleman called Thomas de Granvela got ready for a great adventure. He was going to sail on one of the ships of the Spanish Armada and fight for Spain against England.

Thomas took a gold ring with him, which had belonged to his grandmother. It had her name on it and a date — **Madame de Champagney 1524**.

Later on in the book you will find out what happened to Thomas and his grandmother's ring.

The silver crucifix and gold religious medal once belonged to men who sailed with the Armada four hundred years ago

Why did Spain want to fight England?

King Philip II of Spain

King Philip II of Spain and Queen Elizabeth of England disagreed about religion. He was Catholic and she was Protestant. In those days this made them enemies.

English sailors often attacked Spanish treasure ships coming back from South America. Captain Francis Drake brought huge amounts of Spanish gold and silver back to England and Queen Elizabeth did not punish him.

King Philip's spies discovered that the Queen got a share of the treasure.

Queen Elizabeth I of England

Philip wished that Elizabeth's cousin and heir, Mary Stuart, could become Queen of England. She was Catholic and Philip believed that she would be Spain's friend.

Mary Stuart had been Queen of Scotland. When her husband, Lord Darnley, was murdered her people believed that Mary had helped the murderers. The people turned against her and Mary fled to England.

Elizabeth kept her cousin in prison because she was afraid Mary would plot against her and try to become Queen of England herself. Queen

Mary Stuart, Queen of Scots

Elizabeth knew that King Philip's spies sent secret messages to Mary.

Mary made this embroidery when she was in prison in England

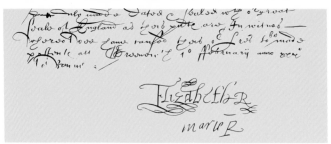

Mary Stuart's death warrant, signed by Elizabeth

At last, when it was proved that Mary knew about a Catholic plot to kill Elizabeth, the Queen sentenced her cousin to death. Mary was beheaded at Fotheringhay Castle in 1587.

When King Philip heard that Mary Stuart was dead he thought of another way to get rid of Elizabeth. He would conquer England and make himself King.

This drawing of Mary's execution was made by a man who saw her die

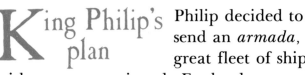

King Philip's plan

Philip decided to send an *armada*, a great fleet of ships, with an army to invade England.

There would be transport ships to carry guns, ammunition and supplies for the invasion force.

Small quick ships would be used to carry messages around the fleet.

Sailors loading an Armada ship. Food, water and other supplies were stored in wooden barrels

But most importantly there must be fighting ships, because Queen Elizabeth's ships would try to stop Philip's Armada landing his army in England.

The fight between the Spanish Armada and the English Navy was going to be the biggest battle that had ever been fought at sea.

The fighting ships of the Armada

One hundred and thirty ships sailed in the Armada. Only sixty eight of these were fighting ships.

The most important fighting ships, called **front-liners**, were the **galleons** and **galleasses**.

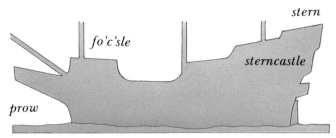

The Spanish galleons had high 'castles' at the prow (front) and stern (back)

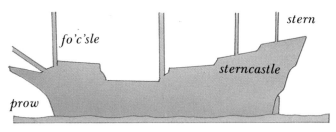

English galleons did not look as big and grand as the Spanish great-ships. They did not have such high 'castles' and they sat 'low and snug' in the water

The Admiral in charge of the Armada was the Duke of Medina Sidonia (left). His galleon, the *San Martin*, was one of the biggest ships in the world at that time.

The great galleon, the San Martin, *flagship of the Armada*

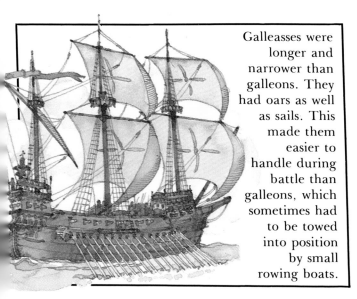

Galleasses were longer and narrower than galleons. They had oars as well as sails. This made them easier to handle during battle than galleons, which sometimes had to be towed into position by small rowing boats.

The **second-line** fighting ships were big merchant ships called **carracks** that were fitted with extra guns. There were forty second-line ships in the Armada.

Armada guns

Spanish galleons and galleasses had forty to fifty guns each.

Big **muzzle-loaders**, 'ship-smashing' guns, were mounted on the gun-deck. They were loaded through the mouth of the barrel and fired heavy shot through the gunports in the sides of the ships.

*Smaller **breech-loaders**, 'man-killing' guns, were fixed on the high parts of the ships and aimed at the enemy crews*

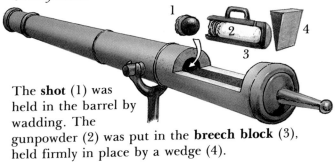

The **shot** (1) was held in the barrel by wadding. The gunpowder (2) was put in the **breech block** (3), held firmly in place by a wedge (4).

Firing a muzzle-loader

1 After each firing the gun barrel was sponged out.

2 The gun was loaded with gunpowder, wadding, shot and more wadding. The wadding kept the powder and shot safely in place.

3 A ramrod pushed each item down the barrel.

4 The **firing hole** was then filled with gunpowder to make a fuse.

5 When the fuse was lit it exploded the gunpowder in the barrel. This fired the shot.

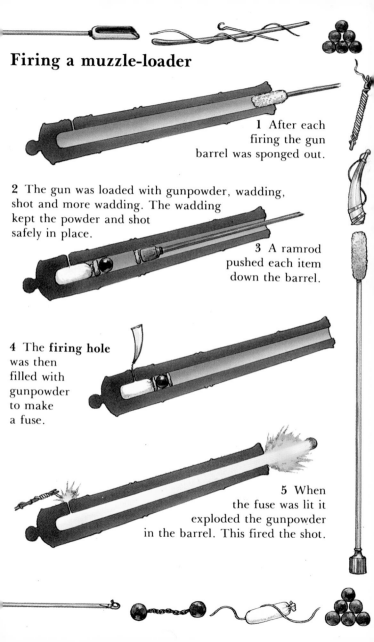

England's ships and guns

News of Spain's great Armada was soon carried back to England by Elizabeth's spies. Although it was such a huge fleet Queen Elizabeth's 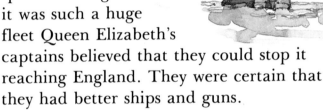 captains believed that they could stop it reaching England. They were certain that they had better ships and guns.

John Hawkins

For ten years a great seaman called John Hawkins had been in charge of Elizabeth's navy. He had built English fighting galleons to a new design. They were faster and easier to

steer than Spanish galleons and could turn round very quickly.

They had more covered deck space so the crews felt protected from gunshot in battle. This extra deck space also meant that the ships could carry a greater number of heavy muzzle-loading guns.

Tools used to repair the ship after battles or storms

15

An English Galleon

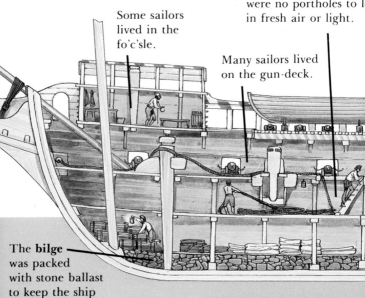

Some sailors lived in the fo'c'sle.

Some sailors lived on the orlop deck, where there were no portholes to let in fresh air or light.

Many sailors lived on the gun-deck.

The **bilge** was packed with stone ballast to keep the ship floating upright.

Backgammon was a popular game during long voyages

These wooden plates from a Tudor wreck were used by ordinary seamen

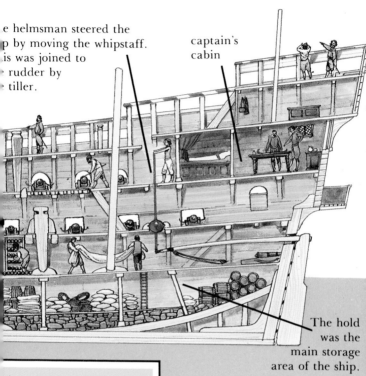

e helmsman steered the
p by moving the whipstaff.
is was joined to
rudder by
tiller.

captain's cabin

The hold
was the
main storage
area of the ship.

A thimble and thimble ring, used to make or repair sails

*A tiny **sundial**, about the size of a 10p piece*

Heavy guns

English heavy guns were mainly **culverins**, which fired shot a fairly long distance. The Spaniards preferred **cannons**. These fired a heavier shot but it didn't travel as far. The English thought that in battle they could hit the enemy using their culverins without being hit themselves.

A Spanish cannon mounted on a large-wheeled carriage. These carriages were very awkward to use at sea

Some of the equipment used by Spanish gunners, including a bucket, a powder scoop, a sponge-head, gauges for checking the size of the shot and a **linstock**.

The English
guns were
mounted on
small truck
carriages with
four wheels.
This made it
easier to load

*An English culverin-type gun
mounted on a truck carriage*

and aim the guns, which could be fired
nearly three times faster than the Spanish
guns.

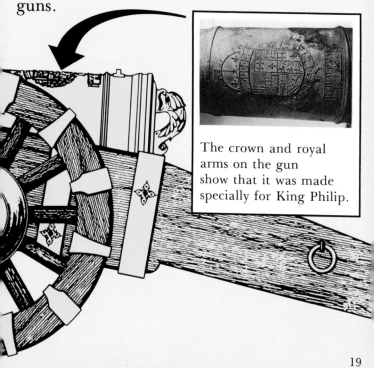

The crown and royal
arms on the gun
show that it was made
specially for King Philip.

The Armada sets sail

At the end of May 1588 the Armada was ready. On board there were more than twenty five thousand men. Among them were two hundred young noblemen who had volunteered to fight for Spain.

Sixty of these young men, including Thomas de Granvela, sailed on the *Rata Encoronada* with a very senior officer, Don Alonso de Leiva.

Fine tableware found on an Armada wreck. It was probably used by officers. The forks are very rare because at that time only rich people used them

Don Alonso gave a grand farewell dinner on the *Rata*. Officers wore their badges of rank and ate from silver dishes. It was probably the last good meal any of them ate for weeks.

The next day the great fleet set sail from Lisbon.

These knights' crosses were worn by Spanish noblemen. The cross of a knight of Santiago (bottom) probably belonged to Alonso de Leiva

Life on board

The Armada ran into storms as soon as it sailed. Sailors were used to bad weather, but the soldiers and young noblemen were very seasick.

The ships were overcrowded, dirty and smelly. Officers and gentlemen lived in the sterncastle cabins. Sailors worked and slept on the upper deck and *fo'c'sle* (forecastle). Soldiers stayed below on the gun-deck.

Few men had beds. They had nowhere to wash and had to use buckets for lavatories on the main decks of the ships.

*Some bowls, jars, a brazil nut and a pine cone –
everyday things that have survived an Armada wreck*

But the most serious problem was the
shortage of food and water. The year
before the Armada sailed, Francis Drake
had raided the Spanish port of Cadiz. He
had burned thousands of good barrel
staves, so the storage casks for the Armada
were made out of unprepared wood. The
food stored in the barrels went bad and
many of the water barrels leaked, leaving
only green slime in the bottom.

With some ships damaged by storms and
many men on board ill from bad food, the
Duke of Medina Sidonia ordered the fleet
back to Spain, to the port of Corunna.

England at last

The Armada stayed in Corunna for a month. Damaged ships were repaired and food and water were taken on board. On 21st July 1588 the fleet sailed again. Eight days later it was sighted off the Scilly Isles by an English ship on patrol.

Sir Francis Drake

Buckland Abbey, Drake's home in Devon

The ship sailed straight back to Plymouth. Legend has it that when Francis Drake heard the news he was playing bowls and said, 'We have time enough to finish the game and beat the Spaniards too.'

Beacon fires, like this one at Golden Cap in Dorset, were lit across England to spread the news of the Armada's arrival

Some beacon sites

That night the warning beacons blazed across England. The next day most of the country knew that the Armada was in the English Channel.

The English surprise the Armada

In Plymouth the English Admiral, Lord Howard, was waiting on board the *Ark Royal* for the Armada. He had with

him about ninety ships. The rest of the English fleet were guarding the Kent coast.

Lord Howard,
Admiral of the English fleet

With Howard were England's greatest seamen and finest ships. There was Francis Drake in the *Revenge*, John Hawkins in the *Victory* and Martin Frobisher in the *Triumph*.

At night, with the wind against them, the English left

Seven days after arriving in the Channel the Armada anchored off Calais

Plymouth and worked their way round behind the enemy.

Next morning the Spaniards were amazed to find the English, with the wind now helping them, preparing to attack the Armada.

The Ark Royal, *Lord Howard's flagship*

The Spanish reply

The Spaniards knew then that they were up against better and faster ships. But the English soon realised that the Armada would not be easily defeated.

At a signal the Spanish fleet formed a huge crescent shape. The transport ships in the centre were protected by fighting ships in front and on either side.

The Spanish 'crescent' in the English Channel. The English dared to attack only the ships at the tips of the 'crescent', for fear of being surrounded

The fighting in the Channel

The first battle was fought off Plymouth. The English had no casualties and the Spanish 'crescent' was unbroken.

For a week the Armada sailed on up the Channel. When the fleet neared possible landing places, at Portland Bill and the Isle of Wight, the English bombarded it, but could not break the 'crescent'.

At last, the Armada reached Calais and anchored outside the harbour.

Fighting between Spanish (red and gold flags) and English (white and red flags) ships

Fireships at Calais

Near Calais an army, led by the Duke of Parma, was waiting for the Armada. If the two forces could join up and cross the Channel together it would mean certain defeat for England. The English had to get the Armada out of Calais before this could happen.

The English fleet sending fireships towards the Armada anchored at Calais

At night they sent eight blazing ships packed with pitch and kindling wood against the enemy. These fireships had no crews to steer them. The wind and tide carried them towards the tightly-packed Spanish fleet.

The Spaniards were terrified. They fled out to sea and scattered northwards along the French coast. For the first time the 'crescent' was broken.

The Battle of Gravelines

Next day, on 8th August, a great battle was fought off Gravelines, a few miles from Calais.

The English fleet, now at full strength, fought at much closer range. They attacked the Armada before the 'crescent' could re-form properly. Their guns did terrible damage.

An eyewitness described one Spanish ship at the end of the day. 'Her decks were a shambles, her guns silent and blood was spilling out of her **scuppers**.'

Many other Spanish ships were in much the same condition. They had few cannonballs left. The Armada retreated northwards.

The English ships were also short of ammunition and had to let the Spanish go.

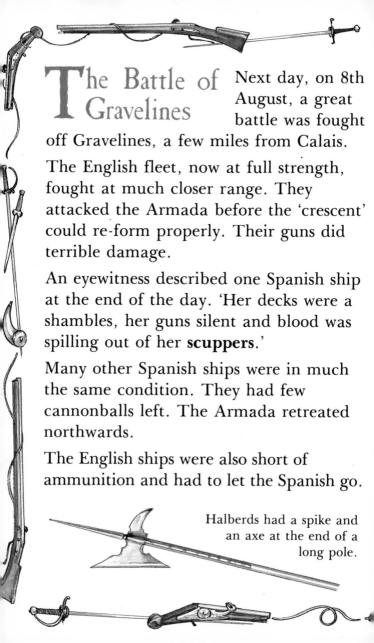

Halberds had a spike and an axe at the end of a long pole.

An armed English seaman, wearing baggy woollen breeches and a leather jerkin. Some seamen also wore simple armour, like the breastplate and helmet shown here.

A Spanish soldier armed with an **arquebus**. Other soldiers would have carried muskets, pikes (poles about 5 m long with a spike at one end) or halberds (see opposite).

Into the North Sea

The English had won the battle of Gravelines but they had not destroyed the Armada.

They followed the Spanish fleet into the North Sea. For a few hours it seemed as if the wind was on England's side. The Armada was blown towards sandbanks near the Dutch coast.

A map drawn at the time of the Armada showing the journey round Scotland

Then the wind changed and the Spanish were able to steer out of danger.

By now the English were running out of food and water and at last, near Scotland, they had to give up the chase.

Queen Elizabeth at Tilbury

In England, people were still afraid that the Armada might return to invade their country.

Queen Elizabeth sailed down the River Thames to inspect her troops at Tilbury. She made a promise that if the enemy dared to land, 'I myself will take up arms, I myself will be your General.'

The soldiers cheered and cheered. Next day the Queen went back to London to wait for news of the Armada.

Queen Elizabeth at Tilbury. This picture is said to have been painted on wood from an Armada ship

The end of the Armada

But the Armada did not return. Too many ships were badly damaged and too many men had been killed or wounded. They had little food, water or ammunition.

*Many Armada ships got lost in the storms because they had only simple navigation instruments like these from an Armada wreck – an **astrolabe**, some **dividers** and a **compass***

The fleet sailed on round the north of Scotland. Their route back to Spain took them out into the Atlantic Ocean, to the west of Ireland.

It was a terrible journey. Fierce storms scattered the ships.

By the end of September only about half the fleet had struggled back to Spain. Many ships were wrecked on the Irish coast. Captain Francisco de Cuellar later wrote an account of how his ship was wrecked.

Captain Cuellar's story

Cuellar's ship, with two others, was caught in a storm near Streedagh, County Sligo, in Ireland. He tells us what happened. 'We were driven ashore. Within the space of an hour all three ships were broken to pieces. More than one thousand were drowned.'

More than twenty Armada ships were wrecked on the west coast of Ireland

County Antrim

County Sligo

This figurehead from an Armada wreck was washed ashore in County Sligo

Cuellar survived by clinging to a piece of wood. After weeks of hardship and danger he says, 'I reached the place where Don Alonso de Leiva, the Conde de Paredos and

The Giant's Causeway, County Antrim, where Thomas drowned

Don Thomas de Granvela had perished with many other gentlemen.'

Cuellar's journey had brought him to the Giant's Causeway in County Antrim.

Dunluce Castle, near the Giant's Causeway, where the survivors of the Girona wreck were looked after

More wrecks in Ireland

Captain Cuellar returned safely to Spain. But Thomas de Granvela did not come home.

With Don Alonso de Leiva he survived the wrecking of the *Rata Encoronada* on the Irish coast. Amazingly they were saved again when the ship which rescued them was also wrecked.

Precious objects from the Girona *wreck*

Then they were taken on board the galleass *Girona*. The *Girona* sank near the Giant's Causeway in October 1588. Don Alonso, Thomas and hundreds more were drowned.

Divers bringing up an Armada gun from the Girona

In 1967 archaeologists found the wreck-site of the *Girona*. On the seabed they discovered many beautiful and interesting objects. One of them was Thomas's ring.

This is the ring that Thomas's grandmother gave to him. It had been lost on the seabed for nearly four hundred years

Victory

The news that many Armada ships had been wrecked in Ireland was sent to Queen Elizabeth. At last, England was certain that the danger of a Spanish invasion was over.

On 24th November Queen Elizabeth rode through the streets of London. The crowds cheered and in old St Paul's Church she gave thanks for England's victory over the Spanish Armada.

This portrait of Queen Elizabeth was painted after the defeat of the Armada. It shows the victorious English fleet and the defeated Spaniards

This medal was made to celebrate England's victory over the Armada. Both sides show the Spanish fleet being scattered by storms

But only the men who had fought against the Armada really knew how much there was to be thankful for. Lord Howard put their feelings into words. 'All the world,' he said, 'never saw such a force as theirs was.'

Drake's drum is still kept at his old home in Devon. There is a legend that says it will beat if England ever faces danger from another Spanish invasion

Glossary

Arquebus
gun carried by infantry soldiers

Astrolabe
instrument used to work out the position of a ship by measuring the height of the sun or stars

Bilge
space between the hull and the hold of the ship

Breech-loader
gun loaded through an opening at the back

Breech-block
removable part of a breech-loader where the gunpowder is placed

Cannon
muzzle-loading gun which fired heavy shot

Carrack
wooden merchant ship fitted with guns and used as a warship in the Armada

Compass
instrument for showing direction

Culverin
muzzle-loading gun which fired medium-weight shot

Dividers
instruments used to measure distances on maps

Firing hole
small hole in a gun barrel filled with gunpowder to make a fuse

Front-liners
fighting ships that lead an attack

Galleass
wooden fighting ship with sails and oars

Galleon
wooden fighting ship with sails

Linstock
wooden holder for the match used to light the fuse of a gun

Muzzle-loader
gun loaded through the mouth of the barrel

Second-liners
fighting ships that act as back-up to front-liners in battle

Scupper
hole in a ship's side to let water drain out

Shot
cannonball

Sundial
instrument used to show the time of day by the shadow of the sun